Fox Gets Help

by Helen Young

illustrated by Shane Nagle

Harcourt

SCHOOL PUBLISHERS

Printed in the United States of America

ISBN 10: 0-15-350343-2
ISBN 13: 978-0-15-350343-6

Ordering Options
ISBN 10: 0-15-350331-9 (Grade 1 Below-Level Collection)
ISBN 13: 978-0-15-350331-3 (Grade 1 Below-Level Collection)
ISBN 10: 0-15-357394-5 (package of 5)
ISBN 13: 978-0-15-357394-1 (package of 5)

2 3 4 5 6 7 8 9 10   179   15 14 13 12 11 10 09 08 07

One day, Fox said,
"Can you help?"

"No," said Cat.
"It is time to eat."

"I will help," said Dog.

"Let's go!" said Cat.

"No," said Fox.

"Dog was the one
that helped."

"Dog can go first,"
said Fox.